YUCK

YUCK'S FART CLUB

AND

YUCK'S SICK TRICK

MATT AND DAVE

YUCK

YUCK'S FART CLUB

AND

YUCK'S SICK TRICK

Illustrated by Nigel Baines

A Paula Wiseman Book
Simon & Schuster Books for Young Readers
New York London Toronto Sydney New Delhi

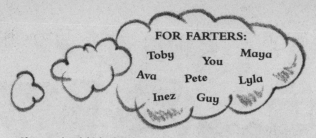

FOR FARTERS:

Toby   You   Maya

Ava   Pete   Lyla

Inez   Guy

SIMON & SCHUSTER BOOKS FOR YOUNG READERS
An imprint of Simon & Schuster Children's Publishing Division
1230 Avenue of the Americas, New York, New York 10020
This book is a work of fiction. Any references to historical events, real people, or real places are used fictitiously. Other names, characters, places, and events are products of the author's imagination, and any resemblance to actual events or places or persons, living or dead, is entirely coincidental.
Text copyright © 2006 by Matthew Morgan and David Sinden
Illustrations copyright © 2006 by Nigel Baines
First published in Great Britain by Simon & Schuster UK Ltd
as two works entitled *Yuck's Fart Club* and *Yuck's Sick Trick*
First Simon & Schuster Books for Young Readers
paperback edition January 2013
All rights reserved, including the right of reproduction in
whole or in part in any form.
SIMON & SCHUSTER BOOKS FOR YOUNG READERS
is a trademark of Simon & Schuster, Inc.
For information about special discounts for bulk purchases, please contact Simon & Schuster Special Sales at 1-866-506-1949 or business@simonandschuster.com.
The Simon & Schuster Speakers Bureau can bring authors to your live event. For more information or to book an event, contact the Simon & Schuster Speakers Bureau at 1-866-248-3049 or visit our website at www.simonspeakers.com.
Also available in a Simon & Schuster Books for Young Readers
hardcover edition
Book design by Tom Daly
The text for this book is set in Bembo.
The illustrations for this book are rendered in pencil and ink.
Manufactured in the United States of America
1112 OFF
2 4 6 8 10 9 7 5 3 1
Library of Congress Cataloging-in-Publication Data
Morgan, Matthew, author.
[Short stories. Selections]
Yuck's fart club ; and Yuck's sick trick / Matt and Dave ; illustrated by Nigel Baines.
pages cm. — (Yuck)
"A Paula Wiseman Book."
"Originally published in Great Britain in 2006 by
Simon & Schuster UK Ltd"—Copyright page.
Summary: In the first of two stories, a naughty boy named Yuck starts an odorous new club, much to the disgust of his sister; and in the second, Yuck goes to revolting lengths to prove that he is really sick on the day of the class spelling test.
ISBN 978-1-4424-8153-4 (hardcover) — ISBN 978-1-4424-8152-7 (pbk.) —
ISBN 978-1-4424-8154-1 (ebook)
[1. Behavior—Fiction. 2. Flatulence—Fiction. 3. Clubs—Fiction. 4. Sick—Fiction.
5. Humorous stories.] I. Sinden, David, author. II. Baines, Nigel, illustrator.
III. Morgan, Matthew. Yuck's fart club. IV. Morgan, Matthew. Yuck's sick trick. V. Title.
PZ7.M8254Ys 2013
[Fic]—dc23
2012027627
yuckweb.com

CAUTION:
YUCKY FUN INSIDE!

YUCK'S FART CLUB

Polly Princess sniffed.

Mom sniffed.

Dad sniffed.

"Who's farted?" Mom asked.

"It wasn't me," Polly said. "I never fart."

"It wasn't me," Dad said. "I almost never fart."

"Well, it certainly wasn't me," Mom said.

Mom, Dad, and Polly looked at Yuck.

Yuck scooped a spoonful of beans into his mouth.

"What?" he said.

"No farting, Yuck," Mom told him.

Yuck chewed his beans.

PARP!

Tomato sauce dribbled down his chin.

BRRAAMP!

"Perhaps you shouldn't have any more beans, Yuck," Dad said.

Yuck scooped another spoonful of beans into his mouth.

He shifted in his seat.

RRRRRRIiiiiPPPPP!

"Yuck!" everyone yelled. "That's disgusting!"

Polly covered her nose and mouth with her hands.

"Right, Yuck! That's enough beans for you!" Mom said, grabbing his plate.

"But I like beans."

Yuck decided that when he was EMPEROR OF EVERYTHING, he would have a swimming pool full of beans. Every morning he would dive into it, swimming and eating and farting, farting and eating and swimming.

"No more farting!" Mom said.

But Yuck had other ideas. . . .

That afternoon his friends were coming around to play.

Polly Princess stood outside Yuck's bedroom door, spying through the keyhole.

Yuck, Fartin' Martin, Tom Butts, and Little Eric were sitting in a circle around a big metal box.

Polly opened the door.

"What are you doing?" she asked.

"Mind your own business."

"What's in that box?"

"Go away, Polly," Yuck said.

"Not until you tell me what's in the box."

"It's a secret. This is a secret club. Go away." And Yuck sat on the box so she couldn't open it.

"It won't be a secret for long," Polly said.

She turned and stomped out of the room.

Yuck waited until he heard Polly's bedroom door click shut, then he gave the signal, picked up the big metal box, and crept downstairs. Fartin' Martin, Tom Butts, and Little Eric followed him through the kitchen and out the back door.

Polly watched from her bedroom window as Yuck and his friends ran down the yard to the tree house. They climbed up the rope ladder and hurried inside.

Yuck was carrying the big metal box.

He leaned out of the tree house, pulled the rope ladder up so no one could follow them, then closed the rickety door.

Polly went to fetch Dad's binoculars.

7

Inside the tree house, Yuck, Fartin' Martin, Tom Butts, and Little Eric sat around the big metal box.

"Is everyone ready?" Yuck asked.

Everyone nodded.

A spider scurried across the floor.

"Then welcome to Fart Club," Yuck said.

He lifted the lid on the big metal box, and a golden-orange glow lit up the tree house. The box was filled to the brim with cold, wet, glistening beans.

Fartin' Martin dipped his hand in.

"Not so fast," Yuck said. "First we've all got to swear by the rules."

"What rules?" Fartin' Martin asked.

Yuck lowered his voice.

"Show me some skin," he said.

He held out his hand.

Fartin' Martin, Tom Butts, and Little Eric placed their hands on top of Yuck's.

"The first rule of Fart Club is—you don't talk about Fart Club," Yuck said.

Everyone nodded.

Yuck continued. "The second rule of Fart Club is—there are no more rules! You can fart whenever and however you want. All agree?"

"We swear on our farts," everyone said.

"Then let Fart Club begin."

Yuck dipped his hand in the box, right up to his elbow, and scooped out a handful of beans. He stuffed them into his mouth. Fartin' Martin, Tom Butts, and Little Eric did the same. They chomped and slurped, chewed and swallowed, handful after handful of beans.

Then they sat back and waited.

"In Fart Club, you can toot, poot, cut the cheese, break wind, drop a bomb, and let off as much as you like," Yuck said. "Just make sure it's big, loud, and smelly."

Fartin' Martin nodded.

Tom Butts nodded.

Little Eric nodded.

Yuck farted.

PARP!

Everyone sniffed. "Phwoarrr! What a STINKER!"

Fartin' Martin farted.

His bottom jumped up and down on the wooden planks.

"I felt that," Little Eric said.

"A BOUNCER!" Yuck said.

Tom Butts lifted his leg in the air and let out a long one.

Little Eric coughed.

Fartin' Martin pinched his nose.

"A GAS PIPE!" Yuck said. "Brilliant!"

"Thanks," Tom Butts replied. He lowered his leg to turn off the gas.

Everyone looked at Little Eric.

Little Eric scrunched his face. He was squeezing.

"I'm trying," he said.

He held his breath and pushed. His face turned red as he squeezed and strained and . . .

"Did it!"

"What?" Tom Butts asked.

"My fart," Little Eric said.

"I didn't hear anything."

"Me neither," Yuck said.

Then they all sniffed.

"Phwoarrr!"

"SILENT BUT VIOLENT," Little Eric said.

PARP! went Yuck.

THRUBADUBADUBADUBA! went Fartin' Martin.

HISSSSSSSSSSSSSSSSSS! went Tom Butts.

————— ! went Little Eric.

They did HONKERS and POPPERS, BLASTERS and SNEAKERS, CRACKERS and SQUIDGERS, but most of all . . . really smelly STINKERS!

And the more they farted the more they laughed. And the more they laughed the more they farted!

The tree house slowly filled with gas until they were sitting in a thick smelly cloud.

"What's going on up there?"

Yuck peered through a crack between the wooden planks. It was Polly.

"Oh, poop!" said Yuck.

Polly was walking towards the tree.

"Quick—start the fans!" Yuck said.

Fartin' Martin, Tom Butts, and Little Eric flapped their arms, trying to get rid of the smell.

Yuck opened the rickety door to let in the breeze.

"What are you doing up there?" Polly cried. She was standing at the bottom of the tree.

"Nothing," Yuck said.

"Well, Mom says dinner's ready, it's time to come in. Drop the ladder down—now!"

"Just a sec."

Yuck ducked back inside the tree house and closed the lid on the big metal box.

"Fart Club will meet again the same time next week," he said. "And everyone bring something with them. We're going to turn up the gas."

He waited for the air to clear, then dropped the rope ladder to the ground.

Fartin' Martin, Tom Butts, and Little Eric climbed down. Yuck came after them, carrying the big metal box under his arm.

"What were you doing up there?" Polly asked.

"Nothing," Yuck said.

"What's in the box?"

"Nothing," Yuck said.

"I don't believe you!"

"I already told you, Polly, it's a secret."

Yuck, Fartin' Martin, Tom Butts, and Little Eric walked back up the yard in silence.

And all the next week, none of them talked about Fart Club. But they were ALL thinking about it, ALL the time: what new smells they could make, what new sounds they could make, and who could do the biggest.

Yuck practiced at night—farting under his blanket.

Fartin' Martin practiced in the bath—making bubbles.

Tom Butts practiced in his garage—filling his bike tires with fart gas.

And Little Eric practiced in the library—letting off silently.

The following Saturday, Polly Princess watched through the binoculars from her bedroom window. With her was Juicy Lucy, Little Eric's sister.

"Why are we spying on them?" Juicy Lucy asked.

"Because they're up to something," Polly

whispered. "They're going to the tree house!"

"Let me see!" Lucy said.

Polly handed her the binoculars.

Yuck, Fartin' Martin, Tom Butts, and Little Eric ran down the yard and climbed the rope ladder to the tree house.

"Yuck's carrying a big metal box," Lucy said.

"I told you!" Polly replied, grabbing the binoculars back.

"What's in it?" Lucy asked.

"I don't know," Polly said. "But we're going to find out."

She watched as the rope ladder went up and the door of the tree house slammed shut.

Inside, everyone sat around the big metal box.

"Is everyone ready?" Yuck asked.

Everyone nodded.

Pill bugs scurried up the walls.

cough splutter must...reach (cough) air

"Then let Fart Club begin!"

Yuck lifted the lid on the big metal box, and the tree house filled with a golden-orange glow.

Handful by handful, they gobbled the beans, sat back, and . . .

"Did you all bring something?" Yuck asked.

Everyone nodded.

Fartin' Martin went first.

He lifted his cap. Underneath, nesting in his hair, was a hard-boiled egg.

"I call this THE FUNKY CHICKEN," he said.

He shoved the hard-boiled egg into his

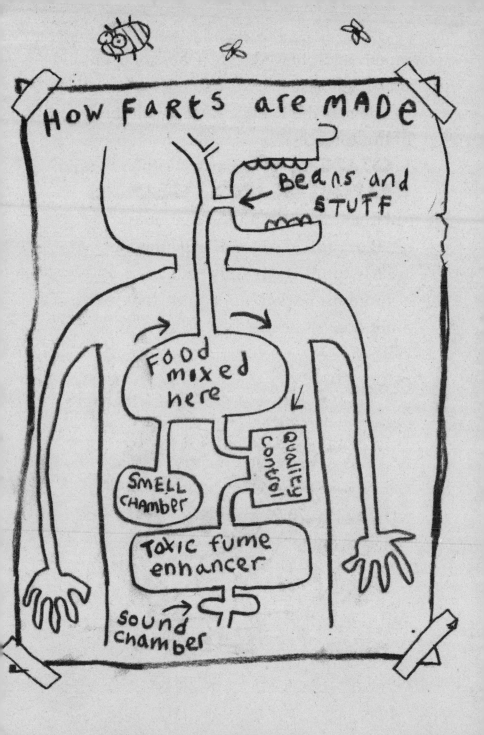

mouth and chewed. Then he stood up and flapped his arms.

The hard-boiled egg mixed with the beans in his stomach.

CLUCK! went Fartin' Martin's bottom. **CLUCK! CLUCK! CLUCK!**

He strutted around the tree house.

"Rockits!" Yuck said, laughing.

"My turn!" Tom Butts said.

From his pocket Tom Butts took out half a hot dog.

"I call this THE DIRTY DOG," he said.

He bit into the hot dog and knelt down on all fours. The beans and the hot dog rumbled in his stomach.

WOOF! went Tom Butts's bottom. **WOOF! WOOF!**

"Let me have a go," Little Eric said.

He pulled out a whole cabbage. It was as big as his head.

"Are you going to eat all that?"

"I call it THE DEAD RAT," he told them.

Yuck, Fartin' Martin, and Tom Butts stared at the cabbage.

"What's a dead rat got to do with a cabbage?" Tom Butts asked.

"You wait till you smell it," Little Eric said.

He munched the cabbage and scrunched his face.

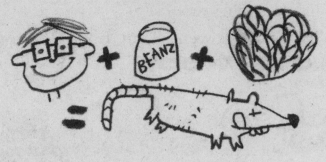

The cabbage mixed with the beans. Little Eric squeezed. . . .

━━━━━━━━ !

A fart sneaked out silently.

"PHWOARRR!"

Yuck, Fartin' Martin, and Tom Butts pulled their T-shirts over their faces.

"Good, isn't it?" Little Eric said.

Everyone coughed. "Dead rats!"

They waited for the smell to die down, then Yuck opened a can of Coola Cola.

He glugged it down in one gulp.

There was a rumbling sound from Yuck's stomach as the Coola Cola mixed with the beans.

"I call this THE BUBBLER," Yuck said.

He lay on his back with his knees up.

He let out a little burp, then his bottom let out a little burp too. Cola-colored gas started leaking from Yuck's shorts. It expanded to form a bubble that slowly rose into the air. Yuck pushed and another bubble burped out, then another. They floated around the tree house.

Fartin' Martin, Tom Butts, and Little Eric reached out and popped the bubbles with their fingers.

PARP! went each bubble as it burst.

Meanwhile, Polly Princess and Juicy Lucy were hiding in the bushes at the bottom of the yard.

"What do you think they're doing in there?" Lucy asked.

"I thought I heard a dog," Polly said.

"I thought I heard a chicken," Lucy said. She peered through the binoculars. "The door's closed. I can't see anything."

"Let's sneak up on them."

"But they've pulled the rope ladder up."

Polly glared at Lucy. "I want to see what's in that box!" She looked at the tree. "If I stand on your shoulders, I could reach a branch and peek through the cracks in the floor of the tree house."

"But what if they catch us?"

"Keep really quiet!"

Inside the tree house, Fartin' Martin was waving a sardine. "I call this one THE SLIPPERY FISH," he said.

He gobbled the sardine in one bite, then lay on his front.

There was a squelching sound as the fish mixed with the beans.

He let out a big wet one.

He shivered and wriggled.

A fart was flapping around in his pants, trying to escape.

FLIPILLOPOLIPILLOPOL

"Are you all right?" Little Eric asked.

"It feels awesome!" Fartin' Martin said, wriggling.

Tom Butts pulled out a bag of popcorn. He opened it and started scarfing it down.

"I invented this at the movies," he said, spraying popcorn everywhere. "It's called THE EXHAUST PIPE."

The popcorn mixed with the beans in Tom Butts's stomach. He squatted, pretending he was holding the steering wheel of a car.

"Awesome!" Fartin' Martin said. His pants were still flapping.

"How about this, then?" Little Eric said.

In his hand he held a raw onion.

"Are you sure?" Yuck asked.

Little Eric raised the onion to his mouth and bit into it. He winced and took another bite. And another.

The onion mixed with the beans.

He squeezed.

Gas crept silently along the floor and up the walls.

Everyone sniffed and their eyes started to water.

"It's called THE STINGER," Little Eric said.

Yuck rubbed his eyes.

Fartin' Martin rubbed his eyes.

Tom Butts rubbed his eyes.

Little Eric wiped away a tear.

"I'm so happy," he said.

"You haven't seen anything yet," Yuck told them. "Watch this!"

Yuck was holding a can of spaghetti.

"Spaghetti doesn't make you fart," Fartin' Martin said.

"This is alphabetti spaghetti!"

Yuck opened the can, dipped his finger in, and swirled the spaghetti letters in their tomato sauce.

He picked out an H, an E, two Ls, and an O, then swallowed them.

He let out the gas. The fart said...

Yuck picked out some more letters, swallowed them, and . . .

WE CAN TALK IN FARTS

"TALKING FARTS! Can I try?" Little Eric said, sniffing.

"And me!" Fartin' Martin said.

"And me!" Tom Butts said.

Yuck, Fartin' Martin, Tom Butts, and Little Eric lay on their backs with their legs in the air.

Tom Butts picked out some letters, swallowed them, and . . .

I'VE GOT A JOKE. WHAT DID THE BURP SAY TO THE FART?

Little Eric picked out some letters, swallowed them, and . . .

Tom Butts picked out some letters, swallowed them, and . . .

Outside, Polly and Lucy looked up at the tree house.

"Are you ready?" Polly whispered.

Lucy nodded.

"Then let's do it."

Lucy knelt down and Polly climbed onto her shoulders.

Little Eric looked through a crack in the floor. He picked out some more letters, swallowed them, and . . .

He pointed downward.

Yuck, Fartin' Martin, and Tom Butts looked through the cracks in the floor.

Fartin' Martin dipped into the alphabetti spaghetti. He grabbed a handful of letters, swallowed them, and . . .

Yuck looked around the tree house. He spied something scuttling up the wall. Swallowing some letters, he farted...

I HAVE A PLAN

Polly was standing on Lucy's shoulders.

"Can you see?" Lucy whispered.

"Hold me steady," Polly said.

"Hurry up." Lucy was clutching Polly's ankles. "I can't hold you much longer."

"I'm nearly there." Polly stretched for the branch. "Just a little bit farther."

But as her fingertips touched the branch, she felt something hairy drop onto her face.

"Uuurrrggghhh!" she cried.

"Stay still," Lucy said.

Polly looked up and saw Yuck sitting in the door of the tree house. He dangled a spider above her.

"Don't you dare, Yuck!" she screeched.

Yuck let go.

The spider dropped.

"EEEEKKKK!" Polly screamed as it fell into her hair.

Then Yuck dropped a caterpillar.

It landed on her nose.

"AAAGGGHHH!"

"Stop wobbling!" Lucy said. "You're going to fall."

But just then Yuck dropped a centipede and a handful of pill bugs. They showered down on Polly and Lucy.

"Get them off me! Get them off me!" they both cried.

Polly wobbled. Lucy wobbled.

"I hate you, Yuck!" Polly cried as she tumbled to the ground.

"Ouch!" Lucy said, crumpling beneath her.

Above them, the rope ladder lowered. Yuck, Fartin' Martin, Tom Butts, and Little Eric climbed down. They were laughing.

"Looks like we've caught a couple of spies," Yuck said. The big metal box was tucked safely under his arm.

"You wait!" Polly Princess told him. "I'll find out what you're up to! And what's in that stupid box!"

"Me too!" Juicy Lucy said.

But Yuck was already walking back to the house.

Little Eric followed behind him. "Fart Club ROCKS!" he said.

"Shhhh, remember the rules," Yuck whispered. "Don't talk about You-Know-What. Next week we'll go for the world's biggest fart!"

And over the following days, no one said a word. But they did leave each other messages. . . .

SATURDAY
AFTER LUNCH
THE TREE HOUSE
THE WORLD'S BIGGEST FART!

And the next Saturday they met again.

Polly and Lucy watched as Yuck, Fartin' Martin, Tom Butts, and Little Eric ran down the yard to the tree house.

Polly had a plan.

Yuck pulled the rope ladder up and closed the door of the tree house.

They sat around the big metal box.

"Is everyone ready?"

Everyone nodded.

All the insects in the tree house ran for cover.

"Then let Fart Club begin!"

Yuck lifted the lid on the big metal box, and the tree house filled with a golden-orange glow. Handful by handful, they gobbled the beans and . . .

Fartin' Martin, Tom Butts, and Little Eric gasped.

At the bottom of the box were a hard-boiled egg, half a hot dog, a whole cabbage, a can of Coola Cola, a sardine, a bag of popcorn, a raw onion, and a can of alphabetti spaghetti.

"The world's biggest fart will need it ALL."

"All at the same time?" Tom Butts asked.

"ALL of it!"

"That'll cause an explosion!" Fartin' Martin said.

"It's called THE ROOM CLEARER," Yuck told them. "The biggest, loudest, smelliest fart in the whole wide world."

"Sounds d-d-d-dangerous to me," Little Eric said.

"You don't have to do it if you don't want to," Yuck told him.

Little Eric shook his head.

Tom Butts shook his head.

Fartin' Martin shook his head.

"You do it, Yuck," they said.

Yuck took a deep breath.

Fartin' Martin, Tom Butts, and Little Eric watched as Yuck shoved the hard-boiled egg into his mouth and chewed. He bit into the hot dog. He munched the cabbage. He glugged the Coola Cola in one gulp. He gobbled the sardine. He scarfed the popcorn. He bit into the raw onion. He winced and took another bite. And another. He swallowed every letter from the alphabetti spaghetti.

BACK INSIDE YUCK'S STOMACH

When he had finished, he lay on the floor of the tree house holding his legs in the air. Everyone waited.

Polly Princess and Juicy Lucy were in Dad's tool shed.

"I've got a plan," Polly whispered. "We'll use Dad's ladder! We'll climb up and catch them."

"And get the box!" Lucy said.

"I'll dash in, grab the box, and throw it down to you. We'll be in and out before they know it."

Polly and Lucy took Dad's ladder from the tool shed.

"Are you okay, Yuck?" Fartin' Martin asked.

"You look a little funny," Tom Butts said.

"Your legs are trembling," Little Eric said.

"Stand back," Yuck told them.

Something bumped against the side of the tree house.

"What was that?"

Fartin' Martin peered through a gap in the wall. "It's Polly and Lucy! They've got a ladder!"

"Get out!" Yuck said. "I'm going to blow!"

"But you'll get caught!" Little Eric said.

"It's too late!" Yuck's stomach was rumbling.

It grew louder . . .

And LOUDER . . .

"Get out! Run!" he said.

Tom Butts flung open the door and threw the rope ladder down.

"Run for your lives!"

Fartin' Martin, Tom Butts, and Little Eric raced down the rope ladder.

As they went down

they passed Polly on Dad's ladder.

She was going up!

"Where are you guys going?" Polly asked.

"Run!" Little Eric said.

"What's going on? Where's Yuck?"

Fartin' Martin, Tom Butts, and Little Eric dived for cover in the bushes.

Polly climbed higher.

Then all at once there came a mighty explosion from the tree house.

A shower of leaves fell from the tree.

Polly's ladder rattled and swayed. . . .

"Help!" she yelled. "Help!"

Yuck popped his head out of the door.

"Don't fall," he said.

Polly clung to the ladder as it shuddered.

Yuck scrambled down the rope ladder and raced to find the others.

"What on earth's going on?" Mom cried, running down the yard.

"Nothing," Yuck said.

"What was that noise? And what are you doing on Dad's ladder, Polly?"

"Yuck's been doing something bad in the tree house!" Polly said.

Mom raced to the ladder.

"Come down."

"But there's something in the tree house, Mom!" Polly told her.

"It's all right, dear, I'll take a look. You come down from that ladder, it's dangerous."

Polly stepped down to the ground.

Mom stepped onto the ladder.

"Oh no," Tom Butts whispered.

"We're done for," Fartin' Martin whispered.

They watched as Mom headed up to the tree house. "If she smells THE ROOM CLEARER, there'll be no more Fart Cl— I mean no more You-Know-What," Little Eric whispered.

"If she smells THE ROOM CLEARER, there'll be no more MOM!"

"I've got it covered," Yuck said.

Everyone watched as Mom climbed the ladder. . . .

For a moment there was silence.

Then Mom opened the tree house door. "There's nothing in here, Polly," she said.

"But there must be!"

Fartin' Martin, Tom Butts, and Little Eric looked at each other.

"Why can't she smell it?" Little Eric whispered.

"There's nothing in here except an old box," Mom said.

"That's mine!" Polly cried. "That's my box!"

"No it isn't," Little Eric said.

Mom carried it down. "Perhaps it's time you all came indoors."

Polly grabbed the box from Mom. "It's mine," she repeated.

As Mom walked back up to the house, everyone followed behind her.

"Look what I've got!" Polly said to Yuck.

"Now your secret club isn't going to be so secret!"

"Give it back," Little Eric said. "It's not yours."

"It is now," Lucy told him, sticking her tongue out.

Polly and Lucy ran into the house and carried the box to Polly's room.

Fartin' Martin, Tom Butts, and Little Eric looked at Yuck.

Yuck was laughing.

Polly sat on her bed and put the metal box on her lap.

"Let's see what's inside," she said to Lucy.

Polly lifted the lid and . . .

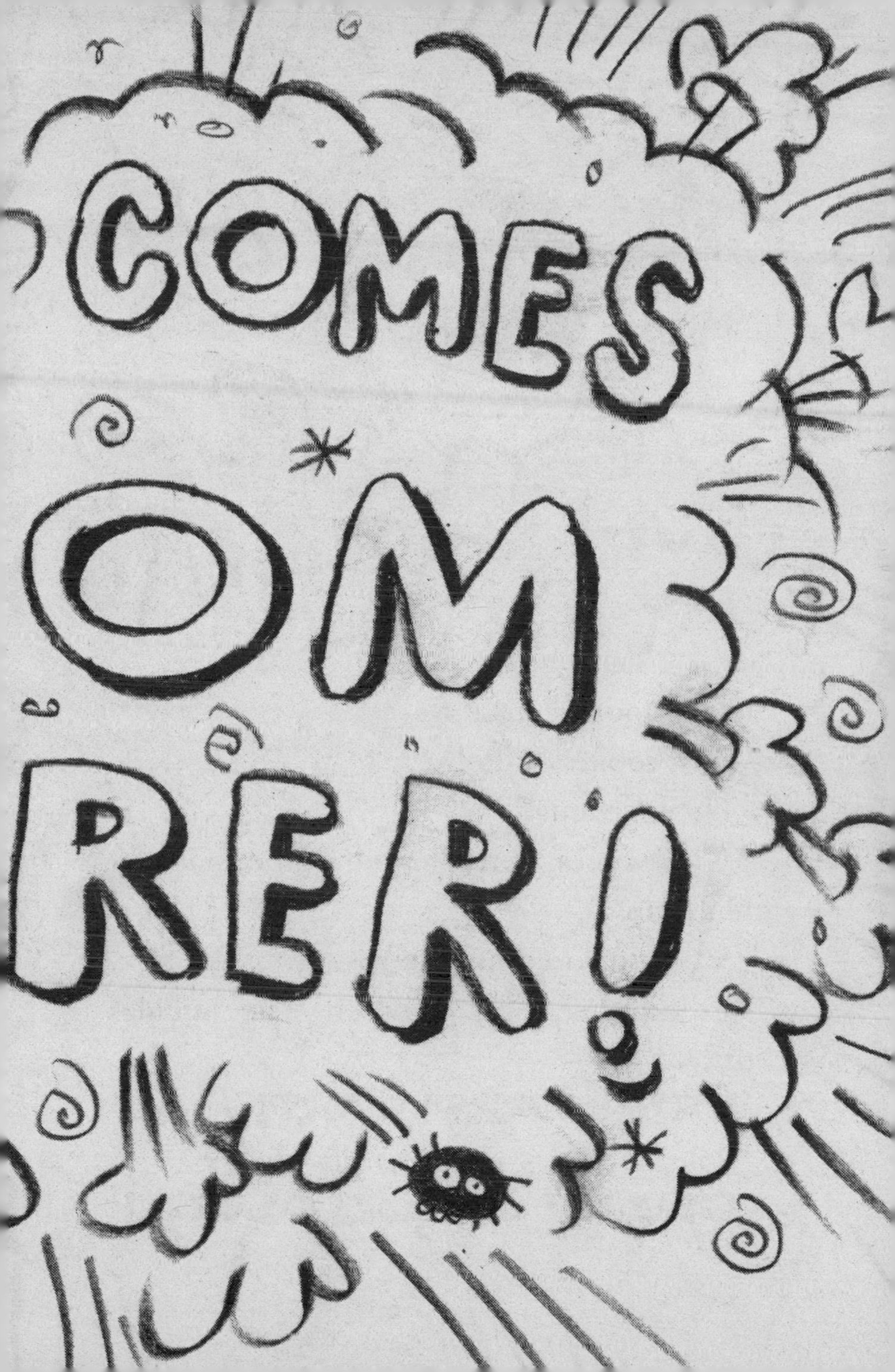
COMES
OM
RER!

CLUCK! CLUCK!

Polly looked at Lucy.

Lucy looked at Polly.

They screamed.

Their noses curled around the sides of their faces. . . .

A cola-colored bubble rose from the box. Then another. And another. The bubbles burst.

PARP! PARP! PARP!

Polly and Lucy could hardly breathe.

CLUCK! CLUCK! CLUCK!

Their throats burned. They coughed and choked.

WOOF! WOOF! WOOF!

It was the worst smell ever!

It seeped into their hair and clung to their skin.

"PHWOARRR!" Polly and Lucy gasped.

The box was steaming.

Something was flapping inside it.

FLIPILLOPOLIPILLOPOL!

They could taste the smell through their teeth.

Something crept out silently.

━━━━━━━━ !

"Dead rats!"

P P P P POP POP POP POP POP POP... BANG!

They covered their ears but there was no escape.

Gas crept along the floor and up the walls.

Their eyes started to water.

"Help!" they moaned. "Help!"

Tears were streaming down their faces.

There was a knock at the door.

"What's going on in there?"

"Help! Help!"

Mom opened the door. Yuck, Fartin' Martin, Tom Butts, and Little Eric were standing behind her.

Mom pinched her nose.

"Polly, Lucy—it stinks in here! Have you been farting?"

YUCK'S SICK TRICK

Yuck opened one eye.

He looked at his clock—half past seven.

Just two hours until school. Just two hours until the spelling test with Mrs. Wagon the Dragon!

I DON'T WANT TO GO TO SCHOOL! Yuck thought.

He pulled the blanket over his head.

Yuck imagined the Dragon leaning over his desk, her eyes black—not just black in the middle but black around the outside too—like deep dark holes.

"How do you spell PUNISHMENT?" she boomed.

She poked him with her umbrella.

Yuck's stomach tightened. He hadn't learned a single word.

The Dragon pushed the tip of her umbrella up Yuck's nose and . . .

"It's time to get up, Yuck," Mom called.

Yuck fell out of bed onto the floor and searched for his spelling book.

He sifted through his *Oink* comics,

through his pants and muddy sneakers, through his water pistols and gunge balls. He brushed the dandruff and plastic spiders from his desk, then lifted the lid and picked through the slugs in Slime City. He ate through the chocolate stash hidden under his pillow. He hunted under his bed, through the mold and mushrooms of Swampland. He

searched his wardrobe—just moths and a bag
of old scabs. Then he stood on his bed and
reached up to the dust shelf—the shelf where
Yuck collected dust.

There it was, half-buried—his spelling
book. Yuck took it down and opened it.

Stuck to the first page was half a cheese
sandwich. Yuck peeled it away and revealed
a list of words.

Library
Grammar
Responsibility
Politeness
Sensible

It's not fair—the Dragon always picks difficult words, Yuck thought.

He looked at the sandwich. A furry green mold was growing on it.

He gave it a sniff.

She never picks good words, he thought, words like YUCK or WART or VULTURE.

Yuck reached to the glass tank on his windowsill.

She never picks words like SNOT or SLIME.

Inside the tank was his smells collection—six rotten eggs, a leaky can of fart spray, a pickled onion, and a pair of smelly red socks.

Yuck held his breath and lifted the lid.

The tank belched a cloud of gas.

Yuck threw in the sandwich and slammed the lid down.

The tank rattled.

She never picks words like FUNGUS or FIB or FOOD POISONING.

Food poisoning! Yuck had an idea.

He stuffed his spelling book behind the radiator and hopped into bed, clutching his stomach.

"AAR, OOO, OWW!" he wailed.

"What's going on in there?" Polly Princess called from the hallway.

"I'm TERRIBLY SICK," Yuck said.

His sister thumped into his room.

"Where's my pink pencil case?" she demanded.

"Go away, Polly, I'm sick," Yuck said.

"I've got art with Miss Fortune today and I need my pink pencil case. Where is it?"

"How should I know? My tummy hurts. My teeth are ch-ch-ch-chattering. I can't even t-t-t-talk properly."

"Stop pretending," Polly said.

"AAR, OOO, OWW! I'm not."

"Yes, you are. You've got a spelling test with the Dragon today, don't you?"

Yuck placed the pillow over his head.

"Go away, Polly. You're making my ears hurt."

"I bet you haven't learned your words," Polly said.

"OWWWW!" Yuck wailed. "I'm sick. I can't go to school."

Polly stomped down the stairs. "Mom!" she cried. "Yuck won't give me my pink pencil case!"

When she was gone, Yuck leaned over the side of his bed and peered underneath.

There, in the middle of Swampland, was Polly's pink pencil case, full of ketchup.

Floating face down in the ketchup was Bonypart, Yuck's glow-in-the-dark skeleton.

"Yuck, it's time to get ready for school!"
Mom called.

The pencil case was Bonypart's blood-
bath. No way could Polly have it back.

Yuck heard footsteps.

He rolled and twisted, yowling and
howling, wheezing and wailing.

Mom came in with Polly behind her.

"Yuck, have you seen Polly's pencil case?"

"Did someone say something? I can't hear.
I've got an earache," Yuck moaned.

"I said WOULD YOU LIKE SOME
CHOCOLATE?"

Yuck peered out from beneath his blanket. "Chocolate! Yes please, Mom!"

"Well, tough, I haven't got any. Now get up and give Polly her pencil case. You're both going to be late for school."

"I haven't got it."

"Liar!" Polly said.

"Double liar. No return."

Polly stuck out her tongue. "I'll get you back," she said. "You wait."

Yuck gulped and gasped and groaned.

"OHHHHHHHH! I'm too sick to argue. I have a headache," he moaned.

Mom opened Yuck's curtains.

"DON'T! I'll go BLIND!"

Yuck scrunched his eyes.

"It's disgusting in here, Yuck. Why haven't you cleaned your room?"

"But I like it like this, Mom. It's full of germs."

"It's gross," Polly said. Yuck rolled over.

"Oh, my head. My head hurts."

"Probably from playing computer games all evening," Mom said.

"And I've got a stomachache."

"Probably from all the ice cream you ate last night."

"And I can't move."

"YUCK! It's time to get up!"

"But I can't move. My whole body's gone numb."

"Well, you don't look sick to me," Mom said.

She whipped back his blanket.

"Don't get too close! I might be sick!"

"Get out of bed, Yuck! And put on some clean underwear! You've been wearing those for a week!"

Polly pinched her nose.

"But they're my favorite underwear, Mom." Yuck scratched his bottom.

"I thought you couldn't move," Polly said.

"Oh, poop!" said Yuck.

Yuck decided that when he was EMPEROR OF EVERYTHING, he'd order a huge pink pencil case to be made— sister-size. Then he'd fill it with cold puke, push Polly in, and zip it up—forever.

"By the time I count to ten, I want you washed, dressed, and at the breakfast table," Mom said.

"But I feel sick."

"One . . . two . . . three . . ."

Mom and Polly went downstairs.

Yuck lay in his bed, groaning.

". . . four . . . five . . . six . . ."

BUT I DON'T WANT TO GO TO
SCHOOL!

". . . seven . . . eight . . . nine . . ."

Yuck jumped out of bed and opened the
lid of his desk. He
took a slug from
Slime City and
wiped it around his
nose. The slug slime dripped like snot, as if
he had a cold.

He opened his
wardrobe and took out
his bag of scabs. He
grabbed a handful,
licked them, and stuck
them to his face.

". . . nine and a
half . . ."

Yuck whipped his clothes on and hurtled
into the kitchen.

"What on earth do you look like?" Polly
said.

"I think I've got a disease!"

"Then wash your hands," Mom said.

Yuck went to the sink, turned on the tap,
and squeezed some soap onto his hands.

Beside the sink he spied the leftovers from

yesterday's dinner. Half a saucepan of spaghetti and tomato sauce. A plate with baked beans and a fried egg in a puddle of yellow yolk. Cold pudding and a bowl of apple crumble and melted ice cream.

Yuck looked around to check that no one was looking. Mom, Dad, and Polly were eating their oatmeal.

Yuck grabbed a handful of cold spaghetti

and picked the skin off the leftover pudding. He scooped up some apple crumble and ice cream, and scraped the egg and baked beans from the plate. He mixed and mashed everything together with his fingers, squishing and squidging, squeezing and squirting, squashing and sloshing!

It felt slippy and sloppy and wet and lumpy—just like puke.

He stuffed the mush into his pants pockets.

"All clean," he said, his pockets squelching as he sat down and helped himself to a big bowl of Monster Snaps.

"I hope these do the trick!"

"What are you talking about, Yuck?" Dad asked.

"I hope these Monster Snaps make me better," Yuck told him.

"Monster Snaps won't do you any good," Polly said. "They're full of sugar and coloring."

Yuck reached for the milk and pushed it over, splashing it onto Polly's lap.

"YUCK!" Polly shrieked.

"What IS the matter with you this morning?" Dad said.

"I'm sick, Dad. My body's been taken over by a deadly disease."

"Then you should eat a healthy breakfast like Polly."

"More oatmeal?" Mom asked.

"Yes, please," Polly said.

"Yes, please," Dad said.

"Oatmeal is disgusting," Yuck mumbled.

Mom placed a small bowl of oatmeal in front of him.

"Come on, Yuck. You must try a little bit."

While everyone was eating, Yuck tipped the oatmeal into his pants pockets.

"I've finished," he said.

Mom, Dad, and Polly looked at Yuck's empty oatmeal bowl. "That was quick!"

Yuck stood up. "Can I play with Furball now?"

He walked over to Furball the cat, who was eating his breakfast by the fridge.

"Yuck! Come and sit down!"

Yuck gave Furball a stroke, then scooped up a handful of cat food.

"Good boy!" he said.

"It's rude to leave the table before everyone's finished," Mom told him.

"But I still feel sick. TERRIBLY sick . . . HORRIBLY sick."

Yuck stuffed a handful of soggy Monster Snaps up his nostrils.

His nose tingled.

"I've got a cold," he said. "Atchoo!"

Monster Snaps and sneezy gunk splattered Polly's hair.

"YUCK!"

"I can't help it," he said. "Atchoo!"

The scabs on his face broke loose and flew across the table.

"YUCK!" Polly screamed. "Mom! Dad! Look what Yuck did!"

The scabs were stuck to Polly's face.

"YUCK!" Dad shouted.

"I can't help it. I'm contagious."

"You don't look sick to me," Dad said.

Yuck stirred the puke in his pockets, then

wiped his hands on the tablecloth.

"You were fine yesterday," Mom said.

"Well, I'm not now. I'll probably have to stay at home and watch television so no one catches it."

"This wouldn't have anything to do with Mrs. Wagon's test today, would it, Yuck?" Mom asked. "Polly told me all about it."

Yuck glared at Polly.

"How do you spell BIG TROUBLE?" Polly whispered.

Yuck jumped up.

"I feel WOOZY! I feel WHEEZY! I feel QUEASY!" he said.

He threw his arms back.

"I think I'm going to faint!"

He fell to the kitchen floor like he'd been zapped by the Xarg.

"Yuck?"

THIS IS WHAT the XARG Look LiKE

Yuck opened his eyes and saw Mom, Dad, and Polly looking down at him.

"What test?" he asked.

"Mrs. Wagon's spelling test."

"The Dragon's gonna getcha," Polly whispered.

"Is that today? I must be losing my memory, too."

Yuck turned toward Dad. He clutched his throat.

"I can't breathe," he croaked.

"You look fine to me," Dad said.

Yuck turned toward Mom. He clutched his stomach.

"I feel sick," he moaned.

"You look fine to me," Mom said.

Yuck turned toward Polly.

"What's that in your pocket?" Polly asked.

The tomato sauce from the spaghetti was oozing out of Yuck's pants.

"I'M BLEEDING!" Yuck shrieked.

He clutched his leg.

"URGH, AAR, OOO . . ."

He rolled his eyes and pretended he was dying.

"He's faking it," Polly said. "He's not sick.

He hasn't learned his words and he's in BIG TROUBLE."

Yuck clutched his heart.

"It's been a good life," he gasped. "I forgive you, Polly. You can have my smells collection when I'm gone."

Mom, Dad, and Polly looked at each other.

"Yuck never lets me near his smells collection," Polly said suspiciously.

Mom scratched her head.

Dad scratched his head.

Yuck lay completely still.

For the first time all morning, Mom and Dad looked concerned.

"Can Polly have your fart spray?" Mom asked.

"Yes," Yuck said.

"Can Polly have your rotten eggs?" Dad asked.

"Yes," Yuck said.

Dad looked at Mom.

Mom looked at Dad.

They both looked at Polly.

"Can I have your . . . smelly socks?" Polly asked.

Yuck gulped. He thought of Polly washing his smelly socks and spraying them with perfume. Then he thought of the spelling test and the Dragon dragging him to the front of the class.

"Only if I DIE," Yuck said.

He closed his eyes.

"He might be . . ."

"He could be . . ."

"He's not!" Polly said. "He's not sick!"

"Perhaps I'd better get the thermometer, just in case," Mom said.

Yuck jumped up. "And perhaps I'd better go back to bed, just in case!"

He ran out of the kitchen and through the hallway.

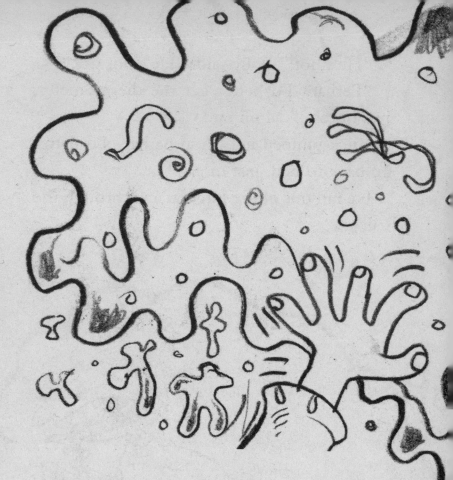

He reached into his pockets, scooped out two handfuls of mushy puke, and threw them against the walls.

SPLAT!

Apple oatmeal stuck to the mirror.

Spaghetti crumble slid down the wallpaper.

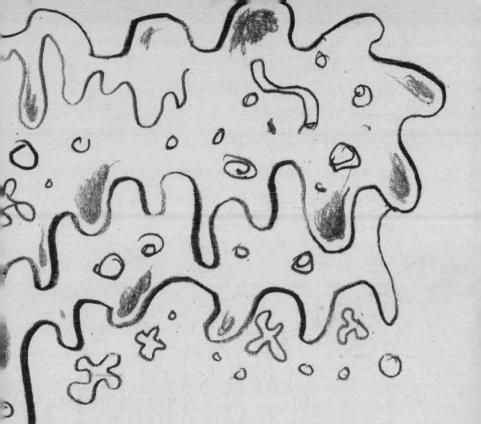

He ran up the stairs, scooped out two handfuls of mushy puke, and threw them against the ceiling.

SPLAT!

Eggy ice cream covered the light bulb.

Fried pudding dripped onto the stairs.

He scooped out two handfuls of mushy puke and . . .

Polly's bedroom door was wide open.

Yuck tiptoed inside.

Beside Polly's bed was her school bag. He opened it. Packed neatly inside were her books and homework. Yuck threw in the handfuls of puke. He turned his pockets inside out, emptying them—cold pudding, oatmeal, and cat food.

Then he closed the bag, giggled, and ran to his room.

Dabbing his mouth with his pukey fingers, he dived under his blanket.

Mom came in.

"I puked, Mom," Yuck spluttered. "It was

horrible. It poured out—everywhere!"

"I think I may have stepped in it," Mom said, looking at her shoe.

It was covered in puke, right up to her ankle.

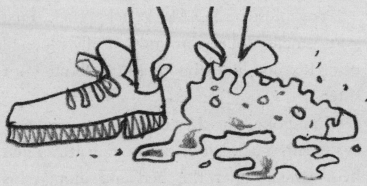

She poked the thermometer into Yuck's pukey mouth. "Keep that there."

Yuck took it out.

"I've been thinking. Perhaps Polly's pencil case is under the sofa," he said. "She always does her drawing in the living room. Why don't you look?"

"You must be REALLY sick, Yuck. First your smells collection, now Polly's pencil case. It's not like you to think about your sister."

Mom poked the thermometer back in. But as she left, Yuck laid it on the radiator. Then he reached under the bed and dipped his finger in Bonypart's blood-bath. He dabbed the ketchup over himself, covering his chest and legs with red spots.

When he heard Mom returning, he got under the blanket and popped the hot thermometer back into his mouth.

"Did you find Polly's pencil case?" he asked.

"She's looking now."

Mom took the thermometer out. Her eyes bulged.

"One hundred and four!" she yelled.
"Yuck, you're virtually dead!"

"I did try to tell you."

Then the door opened. It was Dad.

"I've come to see the patient."

Yuck threw off the covers and Dad and
Mom screamed.

Polly ran up the stairs.

"What is it?" she yelled.

"SPOTS!" Mom cried.

"Chicken pox," Yuck croaked.

"He's already had chicken pox. You can't get it twice," Polly said.

"German measles," Yuck groaned.

"He's had the injection," Polly reminded them.

"French measles, then," Yuck said. "But

I'll be brave. I don't want to miss Mrs. Wagon's test."

"Hopefully, it's something really nasty," Polly muttered.

"Polly!" Dad said.

"Well it would serve him right for taking my pink pencil case."

"Will you be quiet about your pencil case, Polly! Can't you see your brother's sick?"

"But I need it for school. I've got art today!"

Polly stormed out the door and went to her room.

Rockits! Yuck thought.

He lifted one leg out of bed. "AAR, OOO, OWW!"

"What are you doing, Yuck?" Mom asked, tucking him back under the blanket.

"I'm going to help Polly find her pencil case," Yuck said.

"You're not going anywhere," Mom told him.

She looked at Dad. "I'm going to stay and

look after poor Yuck. Can you walk Polly to school?"

"But the test!" Yuck croaked.

Dad went downstairs to put his coat on.

"But I can't miss the Drago— I mean Mrs. Wagon's spelling test!" Yuck said.

"No buts, Yuck. You're far too sick. You're NOT going to school today!"

"Oh well, if you insist, Mom," said Yuck.

Mom puffed up Yuck's pillows, and he snuggled down, smiling.

"Can I have a glass of Coola Cola for being brave?" he asked.

"Of course," Mom said.

"And could you bring the television in so I can watch it in bed?"

"Of course," Mom said.

Yuck was feeling better already.

"Come on, Polly, you'll have to go without your pencil case," Dad called up the stairs. "We don't want you to be late for school."

Suddenly, there came a mighty scream from Polly's room.

"UUURRRGGGHHH!" Polly shrieked. "Someone puked in my bag!"

CHECK OUT YUCK'S NEXT ADVENTURE!